Another delicious tale about Arabel and her pet raven
Mortimer. This time Mortimer takes his trouble-making
to the park. Mum and Dad think that he won't get into
mischief there. How wrong can you be?! The raven is
absolutely determined to have a go on the LawnSabre
that is used to cut the grass. Unfortunately he chooses
the moment that a Round Table and an ancient sword
are found. Could they belong to King Arthur?

OTHER BOOKS IN THE SERIES

Joan Aiken

MORTIMER AND THE SWORD EXCALIBUR

ILLUSTRATED BY QUENTIN BLAKE

BARN OWL BOOKS

Mortimer and the Sword Excalibur was first published by
BBC Publications in 1979
This edition is published by Barn Owl Books in 2005
157 Fortis Green Road, London N10 3LZ
Barn Owl Books are distributed by Frances Lincoln
4 Torriano Mews, Torriano Avenue, London NW5 2RZ

ISBN 1-903015-48-0

Designed and typeset by Douglas Martin
Printed and bound in China for Imago

*Barn Owl Books gratefully acknowledges
the financial assistance of Arts Council England
in this publication*

For Elise

PART ONE

It was a fine spring morning in Rainwater
Crescent, Rumbury Town, north London.
Arabel Jones and Mortimer, Arabel's raven,
were sitting on Arabel's bedroom window-sill,
which was a very wide and comfortable one,
with plenty of room for them both, and a
cushion as well. They were both looking out of
the window, watching the work that was going

on across the road in Rainwater Crescent Garden.

This garden, which was quite large, went most of the way along the inside of Rainwater Crescent, which curved round like a banana. So the garden was curved on one side and straight on the other, like a section from an enormous orange. In it there were ten trees, quite a wide lawn, some flowerbeds, six benches, two statues, a sandpit for children, and a flat paved bit in the middle, where a band sometimes played.

Arabel liked spending the afternoon in Rainwater Garden, but she was not allowed to go there on her own, because of crossing the street. However, sometimes Mrs Jones took her across and left her, if Mr Walpole, the Rumbury Town municipal gardener, was there to keep an eye on her.

Today a whole lot of interesting things were happening in the garden, directly across the road from the Jones's house.

Before breakfast a huge excavator with a long metal neck and a pair of grabbing jaws like a

crocodile had come trundling along the road.
It had started in at once, very fast, digging a
deep hole. This was to be the entrance to an
underground car-park, which was going to be
right underneath Rainwater Crescent Garden.
The excavator had dug its deep hole at the end
of the garden where the children's sandpit used
to be. Arabel was sorry about that; so was
Mortimer. They had been fond of playing in

the sandpit. Arabel liked building castles;
Mortimer liked jumping on them and flattening
them out. Also he liked burrowing deep in
the sand, working it in thoroughly among his
feathers, and then waiting till he was home to
shake himself out. But now there was a hole as
deep as a house where the sandpit had been,
and a lot of men standing round the edge of it,
talking to each other and waving their arms in a
very excited manner, while the excavator stood
idly beside them, doing nothing, and hanging
its head like a horse that wants its nosebag.

While the excavator had been at work
digging, a large crowd of people had collected
to watch it. Now it had stopped, they had all
wandered off and were doing different things in
the Crescent Garden. Some were flying kites.
The kites were all kinds – like boats, like birds,
like fish, and some that were just long silvery
streamers which very easily got caught in trees
and hung there flapping. Mr Walpole the
gardener hated that sort, because they looked
untidy in the trees, and the owners were always
climbing up to rescue them, and breaking

branches. Some people were skipping with skipping ropes. Others were skating on skate-boards, along the paved bit in the middle of the lawn where the band sometimes played. This was just right for skate-boards, as it sloped up slightly at each end, which gave the skaters a good start, and they were doing beautiful things, turning and gliding and whizzing and jumping up into the air, and weaving past each other very cleverly.

Arabel specially loved watching the skaters.

"Oh, please, Mum," she said to her mother who came into the bedroom presently, and started rummaging crossly about in Arabel's

clothes-cupboard, "Oh, please, Mum, couldn't Mortimer and I have a skate-board? I *would* like one, ever so much, and so would Mortimer, wouldn't you, Mortimer?"

But Mortimer was looking out of the window very intently, and did not reply.

"A *skate-board*?" said Mrs Jones, who seemed put out about something. "In the name of goodness, what will you think of next, I should think *not*, indeed! Nasty dangerous things, break your leg as soon as look at them, ought to be banned by Act of Parking-Lot, they should, banging into people's shins and shopping-baskets in the High Street. Oh my dear cats alive, *now* what am I going to do? Granny Jones has just phoned to say she'll be coming tomorrow morning, and your blue denim pinafore at the cleaners' because of that time Mortimer got excited with the éclairs at Penny Conway's birthday party; and I haven't yet made you a dress out of that piece of pink cotton that Granny Jones brought for you last time she came; I'll just have to run it up into a frock for you now, why ever in the world can't

Granny Jones give us a bit more *notice* before she comes on a visit, I'd like to ask? There's the best sheets at the laundry, too, oh dear, I don't know I'm sure –"

And Mrs Jones bustled off down the stairs again.

Arabel wrapped her arms round her knees. She liked Granny Jones, but the pink cotton sounded very chilly; Arabel hated having new clothes tried on, because of the draughts, and her mother's cold hands, and the pins that sometimes got stuck in her; besides, she would much rather have gone on wearing her jeans and sweater.

Mortimer the raven had taken no notice of this conversation. He was sitting as quiet as a mushroom, watching Mr Walpole the gardener, who had gone to the shed where he kept his tools and wheeled out an enormous grass-cutting machine called a LawnSabre.

Just now, this LawnSabre was Mortimer's favourite thing in the whole world, and he spent a lot of every day hoping that he would see Mr Walpole using it. What Mortimer wanted even more was to be allowed to drive the LawnSabre himself. It was not at all likely that he *would* be allowed; firstly, the LawnSabre was very dangerous, because it had two terribly sharp blades that whirled round and round underneath. It was covered all over with warning notices in large print:

DO NOT USE THIS MACHINE UNLESS WEARING DOUBLE-THICK LEATHER BOOTS WITH METAL TOE-CAPS.

NEVER ALLOW THIS MACHINE NEAR CHILDREN.

DO NOT RUN THIS MACHINE BACKWARDS OR SIDEWAYS OR UPHILL OR DOWNHILL.

NEVER TRY TO LIFT THIS MACHINE UNTIL THE BLADES HAVE COMPLETELY STOPPED TURNING.

Secondly, Mr Walpole was very particular indeed about his machine, and never let anybody else touch it, even humans, let alone ravens.

Now Mr Walpole was starting it up. First he turned a couple of switches. Then, very energetically, he pulled out a long string half a dozen times. At about the eighth or ninth pull, the machine suddenly let out a loud chattering roar. Mortimer watched all this very closely; his head was stuck forward, and his black boot-button eyes were bright with interest. Next, Mr Walpole wheeled the LawnSabre on to the grass, keeping his booted feet well out of its way. He pulled a lever, and pushed the machine off across the lawn, leaving a long stripe of neat short grass behind, like a staircarpet, as the blades underneath whirled round, shooting out a shower of cut grass-blades.

"Kaaark," said Mortimer gently to himself, and he began to jump up and down.

"It's no use, Mortimer," said Arabel, who guessed what he meant. "I'm afraid Mr Walpole would never let you push his mower."

"Nevermore," said Mortimer.

"Why don't you watch Sandy Smith?" said

Arabel. "He's doing a lot of lovely things."

Mortimer sank his head into his neck feathers in a very dejected manner. He was not interested in Sandy Smith; and Mr Walpole was now far away, over on the opposite side of the paved central area where the skaters were skating.

Arabel, however, paid careful attention to the things that Sandy Smith was doing. He was a boy who lived in Rainwater Crescent, next door but three to the Joneses, and he was training to go into a circus. He had come out into the Crescent Garden to practise his act, and he was doing tricks with three balls.

He was throwing them up into the air, one after another, and catching them with a hand under his knee, or behind his back, or in his mouth, or under his chin, or bouncing them off his knee, his elbow, his nose, the top of his head, or the sole of his foot; meanwhile he played a tune on a nose-organ which was clipped to his nose.

Arabel thought Sandy very clever indeed, though she could not hear the tune because

of the noise made by Mr Walpole's mower.
But Mortimer was still watching Mr Walpole,
who had now worked his way round to this side
of the garden again.

"Arabel, sweetie," called her mother. "Come
down here a minute, I want to measure you
before I cut out your dress. You've grown at
least an inch since I made your blue."

"*You'd* better come too, Mortimer," said
Arabel.

"Nevermore," grumbled Mortimer, who
would sooner have stayed on the window-sill
watching Mr Walpole cutting the grass. But
Arabel picked him up and tucked him firmly

under her arm. Left to himself, Mortimer had been known to chew all the putty out from the window-frame, so that the glass fell out into the front garden.

Arabel carried Mortimer down the stairs into the dining-room. There, Mrs Jones had pulled out her pedal sewing-machine from where it stood by the wall, and taken off the lid; and on the dining-table she had laid out a long strip of pale flimsy pink material. It looked very thin and chilly to Arabel.

"Take your cardigan off, love," said Mrs Jones. "I want to measure round your middle."

Arabel put Mortimer on the window-sill. But this window looked out into the Joneses' back garden, where nothing interesting was happening. Mortimer flopped across on to a chair and began studying Mrs Jones's sewing-machine.

A sewing-machine was not a LawnSabre; but it was better than nothing. At least it was *there*, right in the room.

"Kaaark," said Mortimer thoughtfully to himself.

Arabel slowly took off her nice thick, warm cardigan.

Mortimer inspected the sewing-machine. It had a bobbin of pink thread on top, a big wheel at the right-hand end, a lot of silvery twiddles at the other end, and a needle that went up and down between the metal toes of a two-pronged foot.

"Mum," said Arabel, when she had been measured, and put on her cardigan again – the cardigan felt cold now – "Mum, couldn't you take Mortimer and me across the road into the Crescent Garden? Sandy's there, juggling, and Mr Walpole too, he'd keep an eye on us –"

"No time just now," said Mrs Jones, through

one corner of her mouth – the rest of her mouth
was pressed tight on a row of pins – "besides,
I'll be wanting to measure again in a minute.
Why can't you play in the back garden, nicely,
with your spade and fork?"

"Because we want to watch Sandy and Mr
Walpole," said Arabel.

"Kaark," said Mortimer. He wanted to watch
the LawnSabre.

"Well, if you want to watch you'd better go
back upstairs," said Mrs Jones. "I'll need you
again as soon as I've sewed up the skirt."

She laid a piece of paper pattern over the
pink stuff on the table, pinned it on with some
of the pins from her mouth, and started quickly
snipping round the edge. The scissors made a
gritty scrunching noise along the table, and
every now and then Mrs Jones stopped to make
a snick in the edge of the pink stuff. Then,
when she had two large fan-shaped pieces cut
out, she unpinned the paper pattern from them,
pinned them to each other, and slid them
under the metal foot of the sewing-machine.

"What are those pieces?" asked Arabel.

"That's the back and front of the skirt," said Mrs Jones, sitting down at the sewing-machine and starting to work the pedal with her foot.

Mortimer could not see this from where he sat. But he saw the bobbin of pink thread on top of the machine suddenly start to spin round. The big wheel turned, and the needle flashed up and down. The pieces of pink skirt suddenly shot backwards on to the floor.

"Kaaark," said Mortimer, much interested.

"Drat!" said Mrs Jones. "Left the machine in reverse. That's what comes of answering questions. Do run along, Arabel, duck; and take Mortimer with you. It makes me nervous when he's in the room; I'm always expecting him to do something horrible."

Arabel picked up Mortimer (who had indeed begun to sidle towards Mrs Jones's biscuit-tin full of red and brown and pink and blue and green and white and yellow cotton-reels, after studying them in a very thoughtful manner). She carried him upstairs, and put him back on her bedroom window-sill.

Across the road, in Rainwater Crescent

Garden, the big excavator was still idly hanging its head, while the group of men still stood on the edge of the huge crater it had dug, arguing and waving their hands about. Sometimes one or another of them would climb down a ladder and vanish into the hole.

"Perhaps they've found a dinosaur down there," said Arabel. "I do wish we could see to the bottom of the hole."

But the hole was too deep for that. From where they sat, they could see only a bit of the side.

Mr Walpole, pushing the LawnSabre, had now cut a wide circle of grass all round the paved middle section. And Sandy the juggler had put away his three balls. Instead he had lit three flaming torches, which he was tossing into the air and catching, just as easily as if they were not shooting out plumes of red and yellow fire.

"*Cor!*, Mortimer," said Arabel. "Look at that!"

"Kaaark," said Mortimer. But he was really much more interested in following the course of Mr Walpole and the LawnSabre. He was

remembering a plane that he had once seen
take off at London airport, when the family
went to say goodbye to Aunt Flossie from
Toronto, and he was hoping that Mr Walpole
and the LawnSabre would presently take right
off into the air.

Now Sandy the juggler stuck his three
torches into a patch of loose earth, where they
continued to burn. He pulled a long piece of
rope out of his kitbag, which lay beside him on
the ground. Looking round, he saw a plane
tree that grew on a piece of lawn already mowed

by Mr Walpole. Sandy ran to this tree, climbed up it like a squirrel, tied one end of his rope quite high up its trunk, and jumped down again. Then, going to a second tree that grew about twenty feet from the first, he climbed up and tied the other end of the rope to *that* tree.

"He's put up a clothes-line," said Arabel, poking Mortimer. "That's funny! Do you think he's going to hang up some washing, Mortimer?"

"Kaaark," said Mortimer, not paying much attention. He had his eye on Mr Walpole and the LawnSabre.

But now Sandy climbed back up the first tree, carrying two of his three torches in his teeth. And then he began to walk very slowly along the rope, holding on to it with his toes, and balancing himself with his arms spread out. In each hand was a flaming torch.

"*Look*, Mortimer," said Arabel. "He's walking on the *rope*!"

Mortimer *was* quite amazed at that. He looked at Sandy balancing on the rope, and muttered "Nevermore," to himself.

"Bet *you* couldn't do that, Mortimer," said Arabel.

However, at this moment Sandy dropped one of his torches, and Mr Walpole shouted, "Ere, you! Don't you singe my turf, young feller, or I'll singe *you*, good and proper!"

So Sandy jumped down again, put away his torches, and went up with a long rod instead. Holding each end of this with his hands stretched out wide apart, he began slowly

walking along the rope once more.

"Arabel, sweetie, will you come downstairs?" called Mrs Jones. "I've sewn up the skirt, and I want to try it on you for length."

"Oh, please, Mum," said Arabel, "I want to watch Sandy. He's doing ever such interesting things. He's walking along the rope. Must I come just now?"

"Yes you must!" called Mrs Jones sharply. "I've a lot to do and I haven't got all day. Come along down at once and bring that feathered wretch with you, else he'll get up to mischief if he's left alone."

Arabel picked up Mortimer and went slowly downstairs again.

Mrs Jones wrapped the pink skirt round Arabel, over her jeans, and then led her out into the front hall, where there was a long mirror.

"Stand still and don't wriggle while I pin it up," she said, with her mouth full of pins. "Stand up *straight*, Arabel, can't you? I want to pin the hem, and I can't if you keep leaning over sideways."

Arabel was trying to see what Mortimer was

doing; she had left him on the dining-room
table.

"Mortimer?" she called.

But while Mrs Jones was pinning up the
skirt-hem, Mortimer was carefully studying all
the pieces of pink material on the table. He
swallowed a good many of them. Then,
deciding that they did not taste interesting, he
flopped quickly across from the table to Mrs
Jones's sewing-machine. Remembering the way
that Mr Walpole started the LawnSabre, by
pulling a string, he tried to start the sewing-
machine by giving a tremendous tug to the pink

thread that dangled down through the eye of the needle.

Nothing happened, except that he undid a whole lot of thread, and the bobbin whirled round and round.

Soon there was a thick tangle of thread, like a swan's nest, all round the sewing-machine, as Mortimer tugged and tugged. But still the machine would not start.

"Nevermore," muttered Mortimer irritably.

At last, after he had given a particularly vigorous tug, the needle broke off, and the bottom half came sliding down the thread on its eye. So then Mortimer swallowed the needle.

Giving up on the thread, he then tried pushing round the big wheel with his claw. Then he tried unscrewing a knob on top of the machine. Nothing happened, so he swallowed the knob. Then he pushed up a metal flap, under where the needle had been, and stuck his beak into the hole under the flap. The beak would not go in very far, so he poked in his claw, which came out with a shiny metal spindle on it; so Mortimer swallowed this too. But as he *still* had not managed to start the sewing-machine, he finally gave it up in disgust, flopped down on to the floor, and walked off into the front hall, just as Mrs Jones finished pinning the hem of Arabel's skirt.

"*That's* done, then," said Mrs Jones. "I'll hem it up this afternoon. Now we'd better have a bite to eat, or that bird will get up to mischief; he always does when he's hungry. Shut the dining-room door, Arabel, so he can't get in; you can hang your skirt over the ironing-board in the kitchen."

Arabel, Mortimer, and Mrs Jones had their lunch in the kitchen. Mrs Jones and Arabel had tomato soup and battered fish fingers. Mortimer did not care for soup; he just had the fish fingers, and he battered his even more, by throwing them into the air, chopping them in half with his beak as they came down, and then jumping on them to make them really squashy.

After that they had bananas.

Mortimer unpeeled his banana by pecking the peel at the stalk end, and then, firmly

holding on to the stalk, he whirled the banana
round and round his head, like a discus-thrower.

"*Mortimer*! You must go outside if you want
to do that!" said Mrs Jones, but she said it
just too late. Mortimer's banana shot out of its
skin and flew through the air; it became stuck
among the bristles of the stiff broom, which was
leaning upside down against the kitchen wall.
Mrs Jones was very annoyed about this, but not
nearly so annoyed as Mortimer, who had a very
difficult time picking bits of banana out from
among the broom bristles.

Mrs Jones refused to give him another.

"When three bananas cost ninety-three
pence?" she said. "Are you joking? He must just

make do with what he can get out."

When they had washed up the lunch dishes and Mrs Jones went back into the dining-room and discovered what Mortimer had been doing, there was a fearful scene.

"Just wait till I get my hands on that blessed bird!" shrieked Mrs Jones. "I'll put him in the dustbin and shut the lid on him! I'll scour him with a Scrubbo pad! I'll spray him with oven spray!"

"Kaaark," said Mortimer, who was sitting on the dining-room mantelpiece.

"I'll kaaark you, my boy. I'll make you kaaark on the other side of your face!"

However, Mrs Jones was really in too much of a hurry to finish making Arabel's dress and tidy the house before the arrival of Granny Jones to carry out any of her threats.

She cut off the tangle of pink thread and threw it all away; she put a new needle and spindle on to the machine, replaced the knob on top from her box of spare parts, set the needle to hem, and put Arabel's skirt under the foot. Then she started to sew.

Mrs Jones's sewing-machine was not new; and Mortimer's treatment had upset it; it began doing terrible things. It stuck fast with a loud grinding noise, it puckered up the pink material, it refused to sew at all, or poured out great handfuls of thread, and then sewed in enormously wide stitches, which hardly held the cloth together.

"*Drat* that Mortimer," muttered Mrs Jones, furiously putting Arabel's pink waistband under the foot to sew it for the third time, after she had ripped out all the loose stitching. "I wish he was at the bottom of the sea, that I do!"

Suddenly the machine began sewing all by itself, very fast, before Mrs Jones was ready for it.

"*Now* what's the matter with it?" cried Mrs Jones. "Has it gone bewitched?"

"Mortimer's on the pedal, Mum," said Arabel.

Mortimer had at last discovered what made the machine go. He was sitting on the foot-pedal, and making the needle race very fast, in a zig-zag course, along the pink waistband.

"*Get* off there, you little devil!" said Mrs Jones, and she would have removed Mortimer from the pedal with her foot, if he had not removed himself very speedily, and gone back to the mantelpiece.

"Mum, couldn't Mortimer and I go into Rainwater Garden now?" said Arabel. "You've done the trying-on, and you needn't come across the road with us, you could just watch to see we go when there's no traffic. And Mr Walpole's there, he'd keep an eye on us. And Sandy's still there doing tricks. And you know you sew ever so much better when Mortimer isn't around."

"I could sew ever so much better if he wasn't in the *world*," said Mrs Jones. "Oh, very well! Put on your anorak, then. Anything to get that black monster out from under my feet."

So Arabel ran joyfully to get her anorak and her skipping-rope, while Mortimer jumped up and down a great many times, shouting "Nevermore!" with great enthusiasm and satisfaction.

Then Mrs Jones watched them safe across the

road and through the gate into Rainwater
Garden.

"Don't you go far from the gate, now!" she
called. "And don't you get near that Bullroarer,
Arabel! I don't want you chopped up, or
squashed flat, or falling down that big hole
it's dug."

"What about Mortimer?"

"I don't care *what* happens to him," said Mrs
Jones.

Part Two

Just inside the gate of Rainwater Crescent Garden, Mr Walpole the gardener was standing, talking to a bald man.

"Hullo, Mr Walpole," said Arabel, running up to him. "Mum says that Mortimer and me are to be in your charge."

"That's all right, lovey," said Mr Walpole absently, listening to what the bald man was saying to him. "I'll keep an eye on ye. Just don't ye go near my LawnSabre, that's all . . . Is that so, then, Mr Dunnage, about the hole? That'll put a stop to that thurr municipal car-park plan, then, I dessay?"

"It certainly will, till we can get someone from the British Museum to come and have a look," said Mr Dunnage, who taught history at Rumbury Comprehensive, and was also on the Rumbury Historical Preservation Society. He then hurried off to Rumbury Tube Station to

fetch a friend of his from the British Museum.

"Seems they found su'thing val'ble down
in that-urr dratted great hole they bin an' dug
just whurr my compost-heap used to be,"
said Mr Walpole. "*I* could' a' told 'em! I allus
said 'twould be a mistake to go a-digging in
Rainwater Gardens. Stands to reason, if there'd
a bin meant to be a car-park under thurr, thurr
wouldn't a-bin a garden 'ere, dunnit?"

"What did they find down in the hole, Mr Walpole?" said Arabel.

"*I* dunno," said Mr Walpole. "Mr Dunnage, 'e said they found su'think that sounded like a sorto' 'sparagus. But *that* can't be right. For one thing, I ain't put *in* no 'sparagus, ner likely to, and second, 'sparagus ain't a root vegetable, let alone you'd never find it down so deep as that."

He stumped away, whistling all on one note, to his LawnSabre, which was standing near the paved part in the middle of the garden.

Mortimer instantly started walking after Mr Walpole with such a meaningful expression that Arabel said quickly: "Come on, Mortimer, let's see if we can find out what the valuable thing is, at the bottom of the deep hole. Maybe it's treasure!"

And she picked up Mortimer and carried him in the other direction.

"Kaaark," said Mortimer, twisting his head round disappointedly.

But when they reached the edge of the enormous hole, even Mortimer was so interested that, for a time, he almost forgot about the LawnSabre. The hole was so deep that a guard-rail had been rigged up round the edge, and a series of ladders led down to the bottom. Standing by the rail and looking over, Arabel and Mortimer could just see down as far as the bottom, where about a dozen people were craning and pushing to look at something in the middle.

"What have they found down there?" Arabel asked a boy with a skate-board, who was standing beside her.

"Somebody said it was a round table," said the boy.

"A *table*? *That* doesn't sound very valuable," said Arabel, disappointed. "I thought they'd found something like a king's crown. Why should a table be valuable? Why should a table be down at the bottom of a hole?"

"*I* dunno," said the boy. "Maybe it's a vegy-table! Ha, ha, ha!" And he stepped on to his skate-board, pushed off, and glided away down the path. Arabel gazed after him with envy. But Mortimer, staring down into the great crater, was struggling and straining in Arabel's

arms. He wanted to go down the ladder and see
for himself what was at the bottom.

"*No*, Mortimer," said Arabel. "*You* can't go
down there. How would you get back? You'd
have to fly, and you know you don't like that.
Come and see what Sandy's doing. He's got his
fiery torches again."

She carried the unwilling Mortimer back to
the circle of watchers round Sandy Smith, who
was now swallowing great gulps of fire from his
blazing torches, and then spitting them out
again.

"Coo, he *is* clever," said Arabel. "How would you like to do that, Mortimer?"

"Nevermore," muttered Mortimer.

He would swallow almost *any*thing, so long as it was hard; but fire always made him nervous, and he edged backwards when Sandy blew out a mouthful of flame.

Then Sandy stuck his fiery torches into the loose earth of a flower-bed, and pulled a wheel out of his kit-bag. The wheel was a bit bigger than a family size pizza, and it had a pedal on each side. Sandy put his feet on the pedals, and suddenly – *whizz* – he began to cycle round and round inside the ring of people who were watching. He made it look very easy, by sticking his hands into his pockets, and playing a tune on his nose-organ as he pedalled along. Then he began to go faster and faster, leaning inwards on the bends like a tree blown by the wind. Everybody clapped like mad, and Mortimer jumped up and down. He had wriggled out of Arabel's arms, and was standing on the ground beside her.

Then Sandy noticed Arabel, standing among

the watchers.

"Hi, Arabel," he said, "like a ride on my shoulders?"

"*Could* I?" said Arabel.

"Why not?" said Sandy. "Come on!"

He stepped off his wheel – which at once fell over on its side – picked up Arabel, and perched her on his shoulders, with a foot dangling forward on each side of his face.

"Hold on tight!" he said.

"*Kaaark!*" shouted Mortimer, who did not

want to be left behind.

But Sandy, who had not noticed Mortimer, got back on to his wheel and began riding round and round in a circle again. Arabel felt as if she were flying; the wind rushed past her face, and when he went round a tight curve, Sandy leaned over so far that there was nothing between her and the ground.

"Oh, it's lovely!" cried Arabel. "Mortimer! Look at me, Mortimer!"

But Mortimer was not looking at Arabel. Very annoyed at being left behind, he had turned his black head right round on its neck and was

looking for Mr Walpole and the LawnSabre. Then he started walking purposefully away from the group of people who were watching Sandy.

"Sandy," said Arabel, as he whizzed round and round, "why are they getting someone from the British Museum to look at the thing they found in that hole, if it's only a table?"

Arabel thought Sandy must know all about it, as he had been in the garden since breakfast-time, and sure enough he did.

"They found a great big round flat stone thing," he said, pedalling away. "It's just about as big as this circle I'm making."

He did another whirl round, and Arabel, who was getting a little giddy, clutched hold of his hair with both hands. Luckily there was plenty of hair to hold on to, bright ginger in colour.

"Why should a man from the British Museum come to look at a big round stone thing?"

"Because they think it's King Arthur's Round Table, that's why!"

Sandy shot off down a path, did a circle

round two trees, and came back the same way that he had gone.

"What makes them think that?" asked Arabel, holding on even tighter, and ducking her head, as they passed under some trees with low branches.

"Because there's a long sword stuck right in the middle of the stone table. And it has a red sparkling ruby in the handle. And they think it might be King Arthur's sword Excalibur!"

Arabel had never heard of King Arthur's sword Excalibur, and she was beginning to feel rather queer. The tomato soup, the battered fish fingers, and the banana that she had eaten for her lunch had all been whizzed round inside her until her stomach felt like a spin-dryer full of mixed laundry.

"I think I'd better get down now, Sandy," she said politely. "Thank you very much for the ride, but I'd better see what Mortimer is doing."

"O.K.," said Sandy, and he glided to a stop beside a tree, holding his arm round the trunk as he came up to it. Then he lifted Arabel off

his shoulders and put her down on the ground. Arabel found that her legs would not hold her up, and she sat down, quite suddenly, on the grass. Her head still seemed to be whirling round, even though she was sitting still.

"I do feel funny," she said.

"You'll be better in a minute," said Sandy, who was used to that feeling.

Arabel tried to look around her for Mortimer, but all the trees and people and grass and daffodils seemed to be swinging round in a circle, and she had to shut her eyes.

"Can you see Mortimer anywhere, Sandy?" she asked, with her eyes shut.

But Sandy had got back on to his wheel and pedalled away; he was juggling with his three balls as he rode.

Meanwhile, where *was* Mortimer?

He was still walking slowly and purposefully towards the LawnSabre, which Mr Walpole had left parked just beside the little hut in the middle of the garden where he kept his tools.

In order to reach the LawnSabre, Mortimer had to cross the paved area where the skaters were gliding about on their skate-boards.

"Watch out!" yelled a boy, whizzing past Mortimer on one wheel. Mortimer jumped backwards, and two other skaters nearly collided as they tried to avoid him. Three more skaters shot off the pavement and ended up in a bed of daffodils.

"You mind out for my daffs, or I'll report

ye to the Borough!" bawled old Mr Walpole
angrily. He had been walking towards the tool
shed to put away the LawnSabre, but now
he stepped into the flowerbed, and began
indignantly straightening up the bent daffodils,
and tying them to sticks, shaking his fist at the
skaters.

Mortimer, taking no notice of what was
happening behind him, stepped off the pavement, and walked on to where the LawnSabre
was standing.

The LawnSabre was bright red. It was mounted on four smallish wheels, and it had a pair of long handles, like a wheelbarrow, and a switch for the fuel, and a lever to raise or lower the blades (so as to cut the grass long or short). At present, the lever was lowered, so that the blades would cut the grass as short as possible.

The motor had to be started by pulling a string, as Mortimer already knew from watching Mr Walpole through the window.

The switch for the fuel was already switched to the ON position. Mr Walpole had left it that way when he went off to talk to Mr Dunnage.

Meanwhile Arabel was beginning to feel a little better, and she was able to open her eyes. She looked around her for Mortimer, but could not see him anywhere. She stood up, holding on to a tree to balance herself, because the ground still seemed to be rocking about under her feet. She could see Sandy in the distance; he was now pedalling about, holding an open umbrella in one hand, and a top hat in the other; he waved the top hat to Arabel, and then put it on his head.

"Sandy, have you seen Mortimer?" called Arabel, but Sandy did not hear her.

"Are you feeling all right, my dear?" said a lady in a blue hat, walking up to Arabel. "You look rather green."

"Yes, thank you, I'm all right," said Arabel politely. "But I am anxious about my raven, Mortimer. I would like to find him. Have you seen him, please?"

"Your raven?" said the lady. "I'm afraid, my dear, that you are still a little bit dizzy. You had better sit by me quietly on this seat for a while. Then we will look for your mummy. I am rather surprised that she let you do that dangerous ride on that boy's shoulders."

The lady obliged Arabel to sit beside her on a bench; she held on to Arabel's hand very tightly.

"Now tell me, my dear," she said, looking round the garden, "what sort of clothes is your mummy wearing? Is she a tall lady or a short one? Does she have a hat and coat on?"

"She has an apron covered with flowers," said Arabel. "But –"

Taking no notice of Arabel, the lady began stopping people as they passed by, and saying: "This little girl seems to have lost her mummy. Will you tell her, if you see her, that I have her child, and am sitting on this bench?"

"Excuse me," said Arabel politely. "It isn't my mother that I have lost, but my raven, Mortimer. He doesn't have a coat, but he is quite tall, for a raven. And he is black all over and has hair on his beak."

"Oh dear," said the lady, "I am afraid you are still feeling unwell, my poor child. Perhaps we had better look for a nice, kind policeman.

I am sure *he* will be able to take you to your mummy, who must be very worried, wondering where you have got to."

By this time Mortimer had climbed up on top of the LawnSabre, and had found the string that was used to start the motor. He took firm hold of it in his strong hairy beak.

Mr Walpole was still crossly propping up his battered daffodils and tying them to sticks with bits of raffia which he took out of his trouser pocket. He did not notice what Mortimer was doing.

"Are you feeling a little better now, my dear?" said the lady in the blue hat.

"Yes, thank you," said Arabel, at last managing to wriggle loose from the lady's grasp. And she climbed down from the bench.

"Then," said the lady, grabbing Arabel's hand again, "we will go and find a nice, kind policeman."

"But I don't want a policeman," said Arabel. "I want my raven, Mortimer."

Just at that moment Mortimer gave the cord of the LawnSabre a tremendous jerk. The motor, which was still warm, burst at once into an ear-splitting roar.

"Kaaark!" shouted Mortimer joyfully.

"Hey!" shouted old Mr Walpole, looking round from his broken daffodils. "Who the pest has started my mower? Hey, you! You get away from that-urr machine. Don't you dare start it!"

But it was too late. Mortimer jumped from the starting-string to the right handle of the LawnSabre. There was a switch on the handle which had four different positions: START, SLOW, FAST, and VERY FAST.

Mortimer's jump shifted the switch from the START to the FAST position, and the mower began rolling over the grass.

"Oh, my goodness!" said Arabel. "*There's* Mortimer!"

And, pulling her hand out of the lady's clasp, she began running towards Mortimer and the LawnSabre as fast as she could go. The Lawn-Sabre, at the same time, was rolling equally fast towards Arabel.

"NEVERMORE!" yelled Mortimer, mad with excitement, jumping up and down on the handle of the mower. His jumping moved the lever into the VERY FAST position, and the LawnSabre began to go almost as quickly as Sandy on his wheel, or the skaters on their skate-boards, careering across the grass towards Arabel.

"You there! You stop that mower directly, do you hear me?" shouted Mr Walpole.

But Mortimer did *not* hear Mr Walpole – the LawnSabre was making far too much noise for him to be able to hear anything else at all. Even if Mortimer *had* heard Mr Walpole, he would not have paid the least attention to him. Mortimer was having a wonderful time. The LawnSabre crashed through a bed of daffodils and tulips, mowing them as flat as a bath-mat.

Mr Walpole let out a bellow of rage. "Stop that, you black monster!" he shouted. "You bring that-urr mower back here!"

But Mortimer did not have the least intention of stopping the LawnSabre. And, even if he had meant to, he did not know how

to stop the motor.

The LawnSabre went on racing across a
stretch of grass which had already been cut
once, and then it crossed the paved strip where
the skaters were skating. The noise made by the
metal blades on the stone pavement was
dreadful – like a giant mincer grinding up a
trainload of rocks.

"Oh, my poor blades!" moaned Mr Walpole,
putting his hands over his ears.

Now Mortimer noticed Arabel running
towards him.

With a loud shriek of pride and enjoyment, he drove the LawnSabre straight in her direction.

"WATCH OUT!" everybody shouted in horror. Mr Walpole turned as white as one of his own snowdrops, and shut his eyes. The kind lady in the blue hat fainted dead away, into a bed of pink tulips. For it seemed certain that the LawnSabre would run over Arabel and mow her as flat as the daffodils.

But just then, luckily, Sandy, who had seen what was happening from the other side of the garden, came pedalling over the grass at frantic speed on his wheel. He swung round in a swooping curve, and just managed to catch up Arabel in his umbrella and whisk her out of the way of the LawnSabre as it chewed its way along.

"Oh, WELL DONE!" everybody shouted.

Mr Walpole opened his eyes again.

Sandy and Arabel had crashed into a lilac bush, all tangled up with each other and the wheel and the umbrella, but they were not hurt. As soon as Arabel had managed to scramble out

of the bush, she went running after Mortimer
and the LawnSabre.

"Stop him, oh please stop him!" she panted.
"Can't somebody stop him? Please! It's
Mortimer, my raven!"

"All very well to say stop him, but how's a
body a-going to set about that?" demanded Mr
Walpole. "That-urr mower's still got half a tank
o' fuel in her; her'll run for a good half-hour
yet, and dear knows where that feathered
fiend'll get to in that time; he could mow his

way across half London and flatten the Houses o' Parliament 'afore anybody could lay a-holt of him. What we need is a helicopter, and a grappling-iron, and a posy o' motor-cycle cops."

But before any of these things could be fetched, it became plain that the headlong course of the LawnSabre was likely to end in a very sudden and drastic manner. For Mortimer and the mower were now whizzing at breakneck speed straight for the huge crater at the bottom of which the round stone table with the sword in it had been discovered.

"Nevermore!" shouted Mortimer, looking ahead joyfully, and remembering the jet plane he had seen take off into the air at Heathrow.

Arabel, running after him across the grass, was now much too far behind to have any hope of catching up.

"Mortimer!" she panted. "Please turn round. Please come back! Can't you stop the motor?"

But Mortimer could not hear her, and anyway he did not wish to turn or stop. With a final burst of speed, the LawnSabre shot

clean over the edge of the huge hole, bursting through the guard fence as if it had been made of soapsuds.

A scream of horror went up from all the people in the garden. And the people who were down in the bottom of the hole suddenly saw a large red motor-mower in mid-air right over their heads, with Mortimer sitting on it.

Luckily there was just time for them to jump back against the sides of the hole.

Then the LawnSabre struck the stone table at the bottom of the hole. There was a tremendous crash; the sound was so loud that it could be heard all over Rumbury Town, from the cricket ground to the pumping station.

The LawnSabre was smashed to smithereens.

The round stone table was crushed to powdery rubble.

But Mortimer, discovering with great disgust that the LawnSabre was not going to take off into the air as he had expected it would, had spread his wings at the last moment, and rose up into the air himself. He did not like flying, but there were times when he had to, and this was one of them.

So all the people up above in Rainwater Crescent Garden, who had rushed to the side

of the hole in the expectation of seeing some
dreadful calamity, were amazed to see a large
black bird come flapping slowly up out of the
crater, carrying a massive metal blade with a
red flashing stone in the handle at one end.

As he rose up, Mortimer had grabbed at the
hilt of the sword which had been stuck in the
stone table; and he took it with him in his flight.

"Oh, if only I had brought my camera!"
lamented Dick Otter, a young man from the
Rumbury Borough News, who had come along

because there was a rumour that King Arthur
and all his knights had turned up in Rainwater
Crescent.

Mortimer was feeling very ruffled. He wanted
his tea. Also he did not quite know what to do

with the metal blade he had brought up with him out of the hole. It was very heavy, and tasted disagreeably of old lettuce leaves left to soak too long in vinegar. Mortimer hated the feel of it in his beak. But he did like the red sparkling stone in the handle. He wanted to show it to Arabel.

Just at that moment Mr Dunnage the history teacher came rushing back with a white-bearded man, who was his friend Professor Lloyd-Williams from the British Museum, an expert in Arthurian history.

The first thing they saw as they ran into Rainwater Crescent Garden, was an open-mouthed, gaping crowd, all gazing up at a rope that was stretched like a clothes-line between two plane-trees.

And on this rope a large black bird was walking slowly along, swaying a good deal from side to side. In his beak he held a long, heavy-looking, rusty sword, with a red stone in its hilt.

"Oh dear," said Mr Dunnage. "That looks like the sword that was stuck in the table. But

how in the world did that bird get hold of it?"

"Well now, indeed," said Professor Lloyd-Williams, "that certainly does look like the sword Excalibur; for a bardic description says that it was 'longer than three men's arms, with a three-edged blade, and three red rubies in the hilt'."

"There's only one red stone," pointed out Mr Dunnage.

"The others might have fallen out," said the professor. "And the bird, no doubt, is one of the

Ravens of Owain, who were supposed to have set upon King Arthur's warriors in battle –"

"How the deuce are we going to get the sword *away* from the bird?" said Mr Dunnage.

Dick Otter, coming up to the two men, said, "Oh, sir, if the sword really is King Arthur's sword Excalibur, can you say what it would be worth?"

"How can I tell?" said Professor Lloyd-Williams. "It is unique. Perhaps a hundred thousand pounds. Perhaps a million."

At this moment Arabel discovered where Mortimer had got to, and standing by one of the plane-trees to which the rope was tied, she called, "Mortimer! Mortimer? Please, I think you had better come down from there!"

By now Mortimer had walked about halfway across the rope, but he was nothing like so good at balancing as Sandy, and he had been swaying about quite a lot. Arabel's voice distracted him, and he now toppled right off the rope, letting go of the sword, which fell point downward, stuck into the ground, and broke into four pieces.

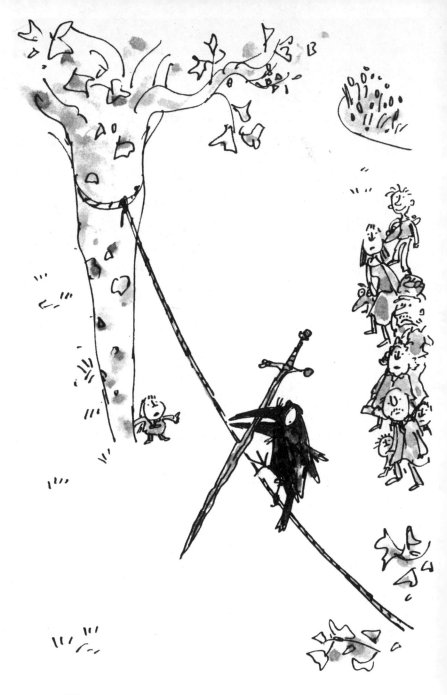

A terrible wail went up from the professor and Mr Dunnage.

"Oh! The sword Excalibur!" They rushed forward to rescue the bits of sword.

Mortimer hoisted himself irritably up from the grass, and looked round for Arabel. In the general excitement over the broken sword, she was able to pick him up and carry him off towards the garden gate.

"I think perhaps we'd better go home, Mortimer," she said. "Perhaps we can get a policeman to see us across the road."

However, just as they reached the entrance, they saw her father, Mr Jones, who had taken an hour off from taxi-driving to come home for his tea.

"Hello, Arabel love," he said. "Your Mum's sent me to fetch you. And you'd best be ever such a good quiet girl at tea – and Mortimer too, if he *can* – because she's rare put out."

"Why is Mum put out, Dad?" asked Arabel, as they crossed the pavement and went through their front gate.

"Because Granny Jones phoned to say she's

got a sore throat and she's not coming after all.
Seems your Ma had just finished making you a
pink dress."

Arabel was sorry that Granny Jones was not
coming, but very glad that she did not have to
wear the pink dress.

"It's lucky Mum doesn't know about your
driving the LawnSabre, Mortimer," she said,
as she went up to the bathroom to wash her
hands before tea. "I don't think she'd have
liked that."

"Kaaark," said Mortimer, who had almost forgotten about the LawnSabre, and was thinking about jam tarts, hoping very much that there would be some for tea. He lifted one of his wings, which felt fidgety, and shook it. Out from under his wing fell the red shining stone from the hilt of King Arthur's sword. It dropped into the washbasin, rolled around with the soapy water, and went down the plughole.

ARABEL'S RAVEN

by Joan Aiken and Quentin Blake

£3.99 ISBN 1-903015-14-6

The first story about Arabel and her pet raven Mortimer. In *Arabel's Raven* Mr Jones, while driving his taxi, notices something bedraggled in the road. Being a kind man Mr Jones stops and discovers an injured raven. Not knowing the consequences the good man takes the raven home and his four-year-old daughter Arabel falls in love at first sight. "His name is Mortimer" she announces and Mortimer has found a home. A series of thefts and a robber squirrel are only two of the dramas in this delightful tale in which Mortimer and Arabel find their way straight to our hearts.

MORTIMER'S BREAD BIN

by Joan Aiken and Quentin Blake

£3.99 ISBN 1-903015-15-4

Mortimer the Raven is causing yet more chaos and mayhem in Rumbury Town. Things get even worse when Arabel takes Mortimer roller-skating with her three nasty cousins Cindy, Mindy and Lindy. But when Arabel gets very ill and is languishing in hospital it is Mortimer who saves her, though some of the other patients have a difficult time – to say nothing of the staff!

THE SPIRAL STAIR

by Joan Aiken and Quentin Blake

£3.99 ISBN 1-903015-07-3

Arabel's Raven is quick on the draw,
Better steer clear of his beak and his claw,
When there is trouble, you know in your bones
Right in the middle is Mortimer Jones!

. . . sang Chris as he strummed on his guitar. Arabel sucked her finger and leaned against an apple tree. Mortimer, Arabel's raven, looked immensely proud that a song had been written about him.

But Chris's serenade was a brief, calm interlude in the tempest of Mortimer's visit to Lord Donisthorpe's zoo.

With Noah the boa using his coils to work the doughnut machine and with the three giraffes all tangled up on the spiral stair, Mortimer's first night in a zoo was one to be remembered for a long, long time.

MORTIMER AND THE ESCAPED BLACK MAMBA

by Joan Aiken and Quentin Blake

£3.99 ISBN 1-903015-24-3

When Arabel and her irrepressible friend the raven Mortimer spend a fun-packed evening with their favourite babysitter, Chris Cross, they have no idea of the chaos they create in their wake.

A reckless game of dressing up and hide and seek results in a number of domestic accidents, a trumpet wedged onto Mortimer's head and a milk shortage.

While Arabel, Mortimer and Chris are out replacing the milk, Arabel's parents return home to find the house empty and apparently ransacked. They fear the worst! Can it be that a black mamba has escaped from the zoo or has Arabel been kidnapped? As police and firemen and anxious ladies comb the streets, the hapless trio, blissfully unaware, are exploring the possibilities of vending machines.

More wonderful slapstick fun with Arabel and Mortimer.

THE BOY WHO SPROUTED ANTLERS
by John Yeoman and Quentin Blake

£3.99 ISBN 1-903015-19-7

When young Billy Dexter tells his friends that he can sprout antlers, he doesn't even believe it himself. Imagine his surprise to wake up with two little bumps on his head that just won't stop growing. Within days Billy has a most splendid set of antlers. No one seems to mind too much, not even the head teacher but there are disadvantages as Billy discovers.

A delightful and humorous tale of difference in a school setting.

JIMMY JELLY
by Jacqueline Wilson

£3.99 ISBN 1-903015-01-4

Jimmy Jelly is young Angela's favourite T.V. personality – so much so that she pretends he's around all the time. Angela's mum and sister can't stand the Jimmy Jelly show but agree to take Angela to see him when the celebrity comes to open a new shopping centre in the area. The outcome is a surprise for everyone.

More wonderful fun from the pen of Jacqueline Wilson.

BOLD BAD BEN THE BEASTLY BANDIT

by Ann Jungman

£3.99 ISBN 1-903015-18-9

Bold Bad Beastly Ben stalks the streets of the town every night, stealing and smashing anything he can get his hands on. As he goes he sings his evil song:

> *"I am Bold Bad Beastly Ben,*
> *I beat the women and eat the men.*
> *Fee-fi-fo-fum,*
> *You'd better watch out, for here I come!"*

Another funny story from Ann Jungmann, author of *Vlad the Drac,* it was originally published in Australia, where it is a great favourite.